RAW 3

HIGH CULTURE

FOR LOWBROWS

Illustrations: Front cover © 1990 R. Crumb. Inside front © 1990 art spiegelman. Inside back © 1991 Kim Deitch. Back cover © 1990 David Sandlin.

**VOLUME TWO
NUMBER THREE**

Editors:
art spiegelman
Francoise Mouly
Associate Editor:
R. Sikoryak
Design Associate:
Dale Crain
Printing:
Freddy Lagno
Aides:
Eduardo Kaplan / Paul
Karasik / Robert Legault
Ed Levine / Steve Marcus
Mark Hurwitt / James Sturm

Published by the Penguin Group.
Viking Penguin, a division of
Penguin Books USA Inc., 375
Hudson Street, New York, New York
10014, U.S.A. Penguin Books Ltd.
27 Wrights Lane, London W8 5TZ,
England. Penguin Books Australia
Ltd, Ringwood, Victoria, Australia.
Penguin Books Canada Ltd, 2801
John Street, Markham, Ontario,
Canada L3R 1B4. Penguin Books
(N.Z.) Ltd, 182-190 Wairau Road,
Auckland 10, New Zealand.

Penguin Books Ltd, Registered
Offices: Harmondsworth, Middlesex,
England.

First published in Penguin Books 1991

ISBN 0-14-01.2282-6

PENGUIN BOOKS

TWO IN THE BALCONY: THE MOUSEUM OF NATURAL HISTORY

Oho! my colleague hard at work! what scholarly readings absorb you with such touching perseverence?

shh...

quiet!

uuhh... nothing... uh... it's a treatise on the paleon~tology of invertebrates... uh... it's a little didactic, but not bad... uh... ...it innerests me 'cuz it's innnerESTing.

I'm referring to the funny-book that's hidden underneath!

if you already know about it, why ask me?

I don't like to be spied on.

if that's your mickey mouse way of cramming for your degree as protagonist in a scientific comicstrip you're in over your head, and I can't reel you in.

I'm reviewing these old funny books 'cuz they're connected to the paleontology of invertebrates. I may get tested on that!

I can't afford to flunk.

just think what your poor mother would say if she saw you reading those trashy funnies instead of studying seriously!...

...and think about our society going into debt to give you a scholarship just so you can piss it away on this illustrated filth!

Translation by Joachim Neugroshol, F.M. & a.s. Lettering by Paul Karasik.

I ONCE MADE SOME CALCULATIONS WITH THE AID OF MY CALIPERS...

...FROM THE MICKEY OF THE EARLY 1930'S TO THE MICKEY OF TODAY THE SIZE OF THE EYES INCREASED STEADILY FROM 25 TO 40% OF THE TOTAL HEAD LENGTH...

...THE HEAD GREW FROM 42.7% TO 48% OF THE BODY HEIGHT, AND THE ANTERIOR DISTANCE FROM NOSE TO EAR INCREASED FROM 71.7% TO 95.6% OF THE POSTERIOR NOSE-EAR DISTANCE!

THIS DATA SPEAKS VOLUMES, DOESN'T IT? DO YOU SEE WHAT DE-DUCTIONS WE CAN MAKE FROM IT?

DEDUCTIONS, EH? WELL... UHM... ASSUMING YOU MANAGE TO DEDUCT THE TRANSPORTATION COSTS OF MOVING SUCH DISTANCES FROM ONE'S YEARLY GROSS IN-COME, THE NATION'S TAX-PAYERS WILL BE ETERNALLY GRATEFUL...

...AND I THINK THAT THIS SUCCESS WILL OPEN THE DOOR TO A FABULOUS CAREER IN COMIC BOOK CRITICISM!

THEN YOU CAN TALK ABOUT MY NOSE AND I'LL FINALLY BE FILTHY RICH AND SUPER-FAMOUS!

DON'T COUNT ON IT! WHEN I BECOME A COMICS CRITIC I'LL TALK ONLY ABOUT MY NOSE. I'LL RUB YOUR NOSE IN INCENDIARY PAMPHLETS! BE WARNED.

NO, HERE'S WHAT REALLY HAPPENED: THE HEAD GREW MORE THAN THE BODY, THE EYES MORE THAN THE HEAD, THE FOREHEAD SWELLED AND GREW AS THE EARS SHIFTED BACK, THE NOSE GOT TURNED-UP, THE ARMS AND LEGS SHRANK AND GOT PLUMP... THESE ARE ALL CHARACTERISTICS OF A JUVENILE: WHILE AGING, MICKEY GREW YOUNG AGAIN!

SKULL OF MODERN MICKEY

SKULL OF MICKEYPITHECUS

MONSTROUS 5-FINGERED MICKEY GLOVE

MICKEY EMBRYO

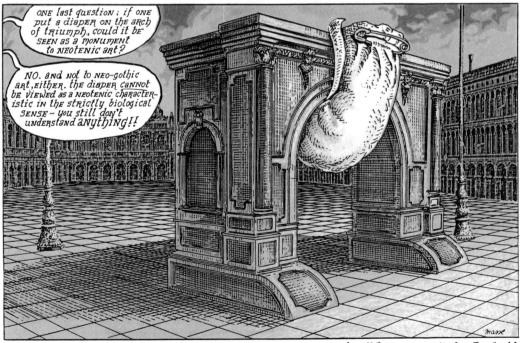

after K. Lorenz and Stephen Jay Gould

MARCEL, THE LITTLE WHITE MAN OF IWINDO

MARCEL WILL GET FRESH NEWS THIS WEEK. CAPTAIN THIVIERE'S LITTLE STEAM-SHIP, "THE ANITA-ROSE," IS COMING UP THE RIVER.

MARCEL RECEIVED A VISIT FROM THE GENERAL MANAGER OF THE LUMBER COMPANY AT THE END OF THE RAINY SEASON. IT WAS FOUR MONTHS AGO AND, IN IWINDO, THE MONTHS ARE LIKE CENTURIES.

"MONSIEUR MARCEL, I BRING GREETINGS FROM MONSIEUR RIOBIQUE WHOM I SAW DOWN THE RIVER TWO DAYS AGO." MARCEL THINKS ABOUT HIS COLLEAGUES WHO LANDED WITH HIM ON THE DARK CONTINENT THREE YEARS AGO, STALKED BY MADNESS, ALCOHOL AND CHOLERA, WHERE ARE THEY NOW?

IS VICTOR SURLY STILL THE POSTMASTER GENERAL IN MATADI? BETWEEN THE HEAT AND THE ABSINTHE, VICTOR – THAT FANCIER OF LITTLE NEGRO BOYS – IS SLOWLY MELTING.

"AS TO YOUR COUSIN, JEAN LEPRETRE, HE ASKED ME TO TELL YOU THAT HE'S HAPPY WITH HIS NEW JOB SHUFFLING PAPERS AT THE GOVERNOR'S PALACE." JEAN HAS NO BALLS ; HE'S NOT A REAL COLONIALIST, AND DOESN'T KNOW ANYTHING ABOUT THE JUNGLE, THE BUSH, OR THE RIVER.

THE CAPTAIN AND MARCEL ARE HAVING THEIR USUAL COCKTAIL – BRANDY AND SODA, NO ICE – WITH THE PIERCING HUM OF MOSQUITOES FOR BACKGROUND MUSIC. THE CAPTAIN WILL LEAVE AFTER THESE ENCOURAGING WORDS:" WHEN YOU GET RIGHT DOWN TO IT, MONSIEUR MARCEL, YOU'RE DOING BETTER THAN ALL OF THEM PUT TOGETHER ..."

MEMORIES OF AN AFRICAN

"SOUVENIR D'UN AFRICAIN"

POURQUOI CES GENS EN OCCIDENT N'ONT-ILS PAS HONTE ? PARTOUT OU JE PASSE, C'EST TOUJOURS PAREIL ET ÇA FINIT TOUJOURS COMME ÇA. ILS NE FONT JAMAIS GRAND CHOSE. QUEL MAUVAIS APHRODISIAQUE BOIVENT-ILS QUI LES AIDE A NE PAS BANDER???

HOW COME THOSE WESTERNERS ARE NOT ASHAMED? EVERYWHERE I GO, IT'S ALWAYS THE SAME AND IT ALWAYS ENDS UP LIKE THIS. THEY'RE NEVER REALLY DOING ANYTHING. WHAT BAD APHRODISIAC ARE THEY DRINKING THAT KEEPS THEM FROM HAVING A HARD-ON?

Chéri Samba's work courtesy Galerie Jean-Marc Patras, Paris & Annina Nosei Gallery, New York. Thanks to B. Jewsiewiski for his translation from the Lingala. Design and translation from the French (trying to keep some of the idiosyncrasies) by F. Mouly.

32" x 23 1/2"

NE LE 30 DEC.1956 A KINTO—M'VUILA LOCALITE SITUEE A MADIMBA DANS LE BAS-ZAÏRE, CHERI SAMBA, DE SON VRAI NOM: "SAMBA WA MBIMBA" FAIT SES ETUDES A L'E.P. ST-LEON DE SA LOCALITE ET LES HUM. PEDAGOGIQUES A L'ATHENEE DE MADIMBA, AVANT DESCENDRE A KINSHASA (CAPITALE DU ZAIRE) EN 1972 OU APRES AVOIR TRAVAILLE CHEZ 3 PATRONS (PEINTRES), CHERI S'INSTALE A SON PROPRE COMPTE LE 10 OCT. 75 SUR L'AV. KASA-VUBU N°89 A KINSHASA/NGIRI-NGIRI. CE FILS DE FORGERON EST AUJOURD'HUI UN AUTODIDACTE DONT LE TALENT A ETE DEJA REMARQUE TANT PAR LA CRITIQUE ZAIROISE QU'INTERNATIONALE. IL TRANSPOSE DANS SES TOILES LA TECHNIQUE DE LA BANDE DESSINEE QU'IL A D'AILLEURS PRATIQUE POUR LE JOURNAL BILENGE-INFO DONT LUI MEME EN ASSUMAIT LA COORDINATION PENDANT 4 ANS (!!!) ...

EN PEU D'ANNEE D'ACTIVITE, CHERI A SU SE CREER UN PUBLIC D'AMATEURS ET A PU SE TROUVER DE NOMBREUSES OCCASIONS D'EXPO. AU ZAIRE ET A L'ETRANGER. IL EST L'UN DES MAGICIENS DE LA TERRE. (1re EXPO. MONDIALE ORGANISEE PAR LE MUSEE NATIONAL D'ART MODERNE A BEAUBOURG ET A LA GRANDE HALLE LAVILLETTE.) IL A PU VOYAGER AUSSI EN AFRIQUE ET EN EUROPE: 1976, 1977 GABON ET CONGO 1978,1980, ENCORE CONGO. 1982, FRANCE & SUISSE. 1984, 1985 SHABA/ZAIRE. 1986, FRANCE & CAMEROUN. 1988, FRANCE & BELGIQUE 1989, FRANCE & ALLEMAGNE (1990, ALLEMAGNE...ETC... SI DIEU VOUDRA)

LA VOIX DU ZAIRE LUI CONSACRE UN FILM INTITULÉ "CHERI SAMBA PEINTRE POPULAIRE!" CHERI EST AUSSI LE COMMENTATEUR DU FILM "KIN-KIESSE?..." ET L'ACTEUR PRINCIPAL DU FILM "MAITRES DES RUES..." DE DUMON-DIRK (BRT).

CHERI SAMBA

28" x 31 1/2"

[Translation of above:] BORN DEC. 30TH, 1956 IN KINTO-M'VUILA (SOUTHERN ZAIRE), CHERI SAMBA, WHOSE REAL NAME IS "SAMBA WA MEIMBA," WAS A STUDENT AT HIS VILLAGE'S PRIMARY SCHOOL, ST. LEON, AND DID HIS HUMANITIES AT THE ATHENEE IN MADIMBA, BEFORE GOING DOWN TO KINSHASA (CAPITAL OF ZAIRE) IN 1972 WHERE, AFTER HAVING WORKED UNDER 3 MASTERS (PAINTERS), CHERI SET UP HIS OWN SHOP ON OCT. 10TH, 1975, AT 89 AVE KASA-VUBU, KINSHASA, NGIRI-NGIRI. THIS SON OF A BLACKSMITH IS NOW AN AUTODIDACT WHOSE TALENT HAS ALREADY BEEN NOTICED BY ZAIRIAN AS WELL AS INTERNATIONAL CRITICS. IN HIS PAINTINGS, HE TRANSPOSES THE TECHNIQUE OF THE COMIC STRIP, A MEDIUM HE ACTUALLY PRACTICED FOR THE MAGAZINE BILENGE-INFO WHERE HE WAS AN EDITOR FOR 4 YEARS.

IN JUST A FEW YEARS OF ACTIVITY, CHERI HAS DEVELOPED A PUBLIC OF PATRONS AND FOUND NUMEROUS OCCASIONS TO EXHIB- IN ZAIRE AND ABROAD. HE IS ONE OF THE MAGICIANS OF THE EARTH (1ST INTERNATIONAL EXHIBIT ORGANIZED BY THE MUSEUM OF MODERN ART AT BEAUBOURG AND IN THE "GRANDE HALLE" AT LA VILLETTE.) HE ALSO TRAVELED AROUND AFRICA AND TO EUROPE:

1976, 1977 GABON AND CONGO. 1978, 1980, CONGO AGAIN. 1982, FRANCE & SWITZERLAND. 1984, 1985 SHABA/ZAIRE. 1986 FRANCE & CAMEROUN. 1988, FRANCE & BELGIUM. 1989, FRANCE & GERMANY. (1990, GERMANY...ETC...GOD WILLING) LA VOIX DU ZAIRE DEVOTED A FILM TO HIM "CHERI SAMBA, FOLK PAINTER!"... CHERI IS ALSO THE NARRATOR OF THE FILM "KIN-KIESSE?"... AND PLAYED THE LEAD IN "MAITRES DES RUES"...BY DUMON-DIRK (BRT).

Chéri Samba's studio in Kinshasa

LAST TIME I WAS TELLING YOU THAT NONE OF THE MATERIAL GOODS IN THIS WORLD ARE WORTH ANYTHING, NOT EVEN CLOTHES. BUT TO SEE THE WAY YOU'RE DRESSED IS REALLY A SHAME. I DON'T UNDERSTAND YOU ANYMORE.

ANOTHER SERIOUS PROBLEM -- LAST NIGHT I WAS FACE-TO-FACE WITH GOD WHO TOLD ME HE WAS VERY ANGRY BECAUSE HE ALWAYS FINDS YOU TAKING A DRINK WHEN IT'S FORBIDDEN TO US. ALL THOSE WHO'LL STOP DRINKING, RAISE YOUR HAND? ONE LAST WARNING! FOR US, IT'S OUT OF THE QUESTION TO FORGIVE THE BAD ONES. ESPECIALLY THOSE WHO STEAL THE MAPAPA (SLIPPERS.) IF I CATCH ONE, HE'S REALLY GONNA GET IT. I'M GONNA CURSE HIM SOMETHING FIERCE. I'M GONNA HIT HIM SOMETHING FIERCE. I'LL PRAY FOR HIM A LOT.

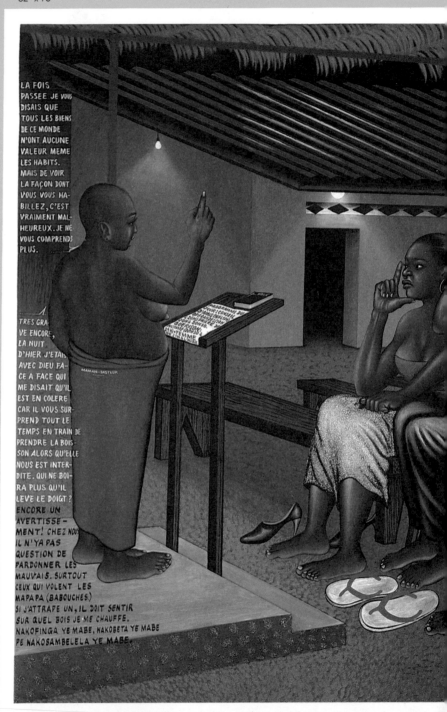

WOOOO!... WY IZ TODAYZ PREECHER TAWKIN' NONSENSE?... WHODO SHE TINK SHE IZ? WHUT DEVIL DUZ SHE FIND IN DRINK?... AN', WHUT DRINK IZ SHE TAWKIN' ABOUT?... IZZIT WATUH? ...TEE?... KAWFEE?... KOKAKOLA?... SKOL [local beer]?... PRIMUS [another beer] ?...

THE SHAMEFUL CONDUCT OF SOME OF
TODAY'S PREACHERS

ARE THEY REALLY WISE OR JUST WISE GUYS? THEY PREACH WITH THEIR MOUTHS, NEVER WITH THEIR ACTIONS. DURING A SERMON THEY ALWAYS TELL YOU: "DO AS WE SAY BUT NOT AS WE DO."

THE SCOURGE OF THE CENTURY

[Top half of circle:] AIDS COMES FROM AFRICA, ALL THE WESTERN MEDIA ARE TALKING ABOUT IT. —ARE YOU KIDDING? WHY IS AFRICA AL–*[continues inside circle:]* –WAYS THE SCAPEGOAT? NO, IT COMES FROM THE WEST, A MISTAKE IN GENETIC ENGINEERING! –WIND BACK THE CLOCK *[bottom of circle:]* BUT... WHAT'S THE POINT OF SUCH ENDLESS ARGUMENTS? WHAT ARE THE RESEARCHERS DOING? DON'T WE HAVE THE RIGHT TO LIVE?

22" x 25 1/2"

IL N'Y AURA JAMAIS DE MAUVAIS OUVRIERS AU MONDE SI LES PATRONS AURONT DES MAINS CHARITABLES

LOVE OF WORK

I LOVE MY WORK. UNFORTUNATELY, I ALWAYS RUN INTO PEOPLE WHO, WITH THEIR STRANGLEHOLD ON ME, EARN A LIVING ON MY BACK.

THERE NEVER WILL BE BAD WORKERS IN THE WORLD IF THE BOSSES' HANDS WERE MORE CHARITABLE.

THE BATTLE AGAINST THE MOSQUITOES

-- YOU KILL THOSE ON THE RIGHT, DARLING, WHILE I FIGHT THE LEFTISTS.

-- I'M DOING IT, MY LOVE. I ALREADY KILLED TWO BUT IT SEEMS TO ME THAT THEY'RE COMING BACK TO LIFE.

CAREFUL!.. CAREFUL!.. ALL THE MEANS OF AIDS TRANSMISSION ARE NOT YET KNOWN, AND THE DISEASE ITSELF IS STILL INCURABLE SO FAR. LOVERS HAVE A PROBLEM. THEY MUST KNOW WHERE IT'S SAFE TO THROW AWAY USED CONDOMS

52" x 79"

25 3/8" x 31 1/2"

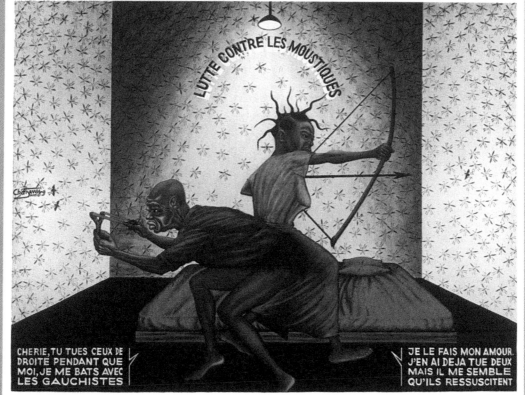

EN AFRIQUE, LA MALARIA TUE PLUS QUE LE SIDA. SURTOUT CHEZ LES PETITS ENFANTS. LE VIRUS DE LA MALARIA S'APPELE "MOUSTIQUES." CE VIRUS SEMBLE ETRE TRES PUISSANT QUE LES BLANCS ET LES NOIRS QUI VIVENT EN AFRIQUE

IN AFRICA, MALARIA KILLS MORE THAN AIDS. ESPECIALLY AMONG SMALL CHILDREN. THE VIRUS OF MALARIA IS CALLED "MOSQUITO." THIS VIRUS SEEMS TO BE MORE POWERFUL THAN WHITES AND BLACKS LIVING IN AFRICA.

1. IT'S TRUE THAT IT'S HARD TO EARN MONEY. I SPENT A LOT OF TIME IN THIS FOREIGN COUNTRY BUT I HAVEN'T EARNED MUCH. BETTER GO HOME BEFORE I RUN OUT OF THE LITTLE BIT I EARNED. BUT... IN THE COUNTRY I'M GOING BACK TO, THERE'RE TOO MANY PROBLEMS. I DON'T KNOW IF THE MEMBERS OF THE **SO·PE·KA** (BUY-GIVE-SHARE) ARE STILL AROUND.

2. FRANKLY, AT HOME WE TAKE MONEY FOR GRANTED. FROM THE 1ST TO THE 31ST WE'RE ALWAYS ASKING FOR HELP. THIS TIME THE FLATTERERS WILL RESENT ME. I WON'T MAKE THE MISTAKE AGAIN OF THROWING MONEY AROUND. I'LL EVEN ENDURE THE PAIN OF TRAVELING EVERYWHERE BY FOOT. A BIT OF LAND IS THE THING. I'VE GOT TO GET A BIT OF LAND OTHERWISE I'LL ALWAYS BE A TENANT.

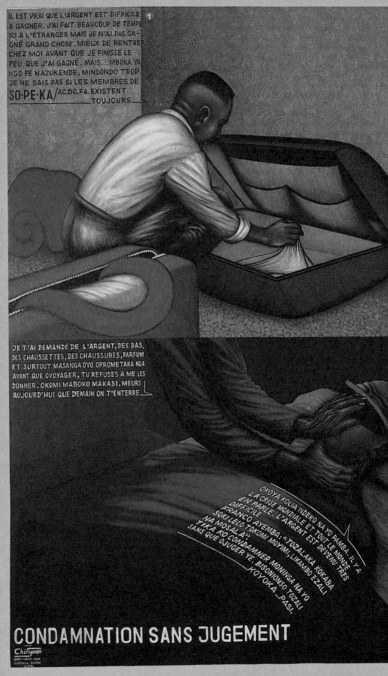

4. I ASKED YOU FOR MONEY, STOCKINGS, SOCKS, SHOES, PERFUME AND ESPECIALLY FOR THE BEER YOU PROMISED ME BEFORE GOING ON YOUR TRIP. YOU REFUSE TO GIVE THEM TO ME. YOU'RE TIGHT-FISTED. DIE TODAY SO WE BURY YOU TOMORROW.

YOU'RE ABOUT TO PREY ON YOUR BROTHER FOR NOTHING. THERE'S A WORLD CRISIS GOING ON. THE WHOLE WORLD IS TALKING ABOUT IT. MONEY HAS BECOME VERY HARD TO GET. "WE USED TO SHARE; IF TODAY WE'VE BECOME TIGHT-FISTED, IT'S BECAUSE OF SOMETHING AT OUR JOBS." DON'T CONDEMN YOUR FRIEND WITHOUT A TRIAL. ALL OF US ARE IN TROUBLE.

CONDEMNED WITHOUT A TRIAL

3. **LOCAL COMMITTEE OF BEGGARS**
A DECENTRALIZED COMMITTEE WHOSE MOTTO IS: SO-PE-KA
BUY ME -GIVE ME-SHARE WITH ME

FLATTERERS ASSOCIATION A FOR-PROFIT ORGANIZATION
WELCOMES YOU. DON'T FORGET OUR MOTTO: SO-PE-KA
IF YOU GIVE TO SOMEONE ONCE, YOU HAVE TO DO IT EVERY TIME OR YOU'LL BE SEEN AS STINGY.

I'M DELIGHTED TO SEE YOU AND I HOPE ALL MY PROBLEMS ARE GOING TO BE SOLVED. GIVE ME THE MONEY. WHERE IS THE BEER?

CAN'T YOU GIVE *ME* SOMETHING? EVERY DAY, YOU'RE ALWAYS ASKING FOR SOMETHING. WHY AREN'T YOU ASHAMED? LEAVE ME ALONE, I DON'T HAVE A LOT.

5. FLATTERY IS BAD... TO SOLVE THE WORLD CRISIS, DON'T DEPEND ON THE EFFORTS OF JUST ONE PERSON. NOWADAYS, PEOPLE LIKE THE EASY LIFE BUT THEY FORGET ABOUT WORK. THEY JUST PESTER SOMEONE ELSE. "HELPING" HAS BECOME ALMOST MYSTICAL. THE ANCESTORS SAID: "HE WHO EATS WITH YOU IS YOUR ENEMY. THE FLATTERER NEVER APPRECIATES ANYONE; IT MAKES NO DIFFERENCE IF YOU GIVE OR NOT. THE DAY YOU FALL, HE WON'T COME TO YOUR AID; RATHER IT WILL BE HIM WHO WILL LAUGH AT YOU."

IN A CORNER OF A FULLY-AUTOMATED FACTORY ON A PLANET ENFOLDED WITHIN A CARTOON SURREALIST GALAXY, A BIG MEAN BASTARD MACHINE CHUGS AWAY AS IT HAS FOR A HUNDRED MILLION YEARS.

NOTHING BROKEN.

I'D. BETTER GET BACK ON.

BUT THE MACHINE HAD CLOSED RANKS

MY SPOT'S GONE! WHAT DO I DO NOW?

THIS PLACE IS HUGE!

THE LITTLE BASTARD ROAMED AROUND IN THE FACTORY FOR DAYS AND DAYS WITHOUT A SIGN OF ANYONE ---

UNTIL HE FOUND HIMSELF

OUT

SIDE

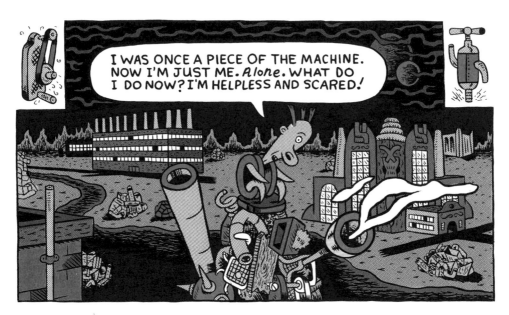

KRAZY KAT

In May of 1936, the author of **Krazy Kat**, George Herriman, abandoned his whimsical lyricism for about eight weeks in order to compose a rare sustained Krazy Kat narrative involving this rather remarkable **Tiger Tea**, which properties my generation has long associated with marijuana, and Mr. Segar's generation has long associated with spinach.

"Tiger Tea" is Herriman's own flirtation with high-adventure Continuity as it first blasted onto Depression-era newspaper pages and surrounded Krazy with Tarzan, Tracy, Buck Rogers and the rest. "Tiger Tea," as rescored here from a four-panel daily into six-panel comic book pages, finds Herriman riding a wild river composed of his own fabulous ethnic dialecticisms. It includes some of Herriman's very best writing (his <u>only</u> writing at a stretch). George's strange yiddisha ragtime dickensian voice has never sung quite so sweetly.   -Bob Callahan

Bob Callahan is the executive editor and co-publisher of **The Komplete Kat Komics**, now in its seventh volume from Eclipse Books/Turtle Island (PO Box 1099, Forestville, Ca. 95436)

For further reading see also:**The Komplete Kolor Krazy Kat** edited by Rick Marschall, Remco World Service Books (from Kitchen Sink Press, 2 Swamp Road, Princeton, Wi. 54968) & **The Comic Art of George Herriman** by Patrick McDonnell et. al., Abrams, NY.

HERRIMAN

7-4

2

3   7-6   4

NORTH AMERICANS

Translation by Eduardo Kaplan. Lettering by Phil Felix. © 1988 Jose Muñoz & Carlos Sampayo

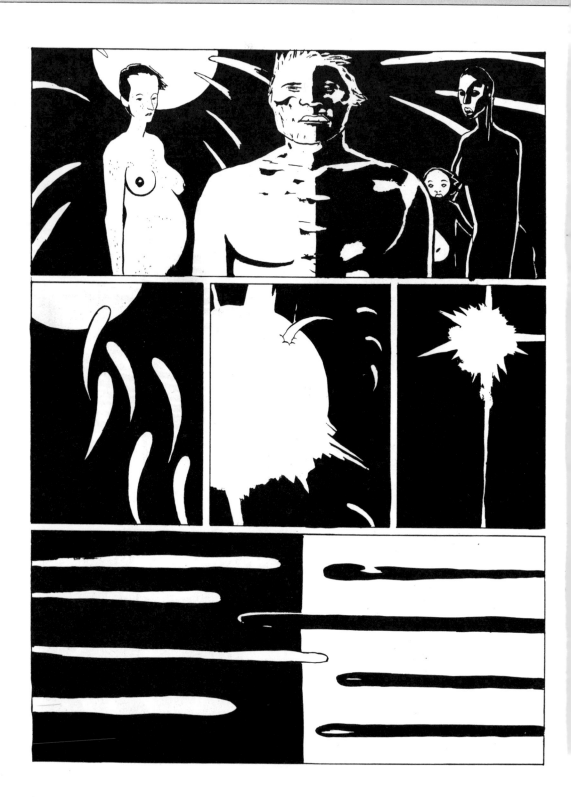

* THEY'RE REALLY HOSPITABLE AROUND HERE, AREN'T THEY?

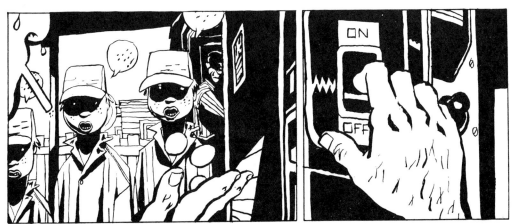

I,...
...I'LL
PRESS
CHARGES...

YEAH. AND THEY DE-
SERVE IT...BUT THE
PLATES ARE FROM
ANOTHER
STATE...
YOU
KNOW
HOW
IT IS...

...MY HANDS ARE TIED, SIR. BUT IF YOU NEED ANYTHING ELSE, PLEASE DON'T HESITATE TO ASK.

I NEED WATER. BUT THERE DOESN'T SEEM TO BE ANY IN THIS TOWN.

VERY FUNNY... ANYTHING ELSE?

HE'S STILL AROUND...

...MAYBE HE LIKES IT...

Señor Mort...!

WHAT ARE YOU DOING?

END

I REMEMBER PEGGY

ME / PEGGY

By Aline Goldsmith-Crumb '90

Spring 1990... watching TWIN PEAKS on TV

HEY GUYS.. I KNOW HER.... THAT'S PEGGY LIPTON.. I WENT TO HIGH SCHOOL WITH HER...

S'MORE COFFEE ED?

SURE NORMA

SHE STILL LOOKS FABULOUS AN' SHE'S A YEAR OLDER THAN ME.. NO WRINKLES!

I HATE THE WAY SHE LOOKS. SHE'S TOO SKINNY! I HOPE YOU DON'T WANNA BE LIKE HER!

HOW COME SHE SEEMS YOUNGER THAN YOU MOMMY? DID SHE GET A FACE JOB?

LOUSY ACTRESS

HOW CAN HE SAY THAT?! TO ME SHE WAS PERFECT.

I CLEARLY REMEMBER HER.

SHE WAS ONE OF US...

AND YET..

IT WAS 1965 IN CEDARHURST, LONG ISLAND ....

WE HAD PROBLEMS..

LARGE NOSES

BRACES

HIPS

PAPAGALLO SHOES A MUST.

BIG HAIR HARD TO CONTROL

OILY SKIN

FIRE PLUG PHYSIQUES

PUSHY PERSONALITIES

NOT PERKY OR DREAMY ENUFF!

WE TRIED TO WORK WITH OUR FLAWS...

HAIR IRONING

CONTACT LENSES

PANTY GIRDLE

RHINO-PLASTY

DARK STOCKINGS

CHIN JOB

POINTY SHOES TO ELONGATE LEGS

DERMA-BRASION

AND WE MIGHT HAVE ACCEPTED OUR FATE AS GENETIC DESTINY MORE EASILY IF ONLY ....

PEGGY

SHE'S A GODDESS I WISH I COULD BE HER. SHE'S SO ABOVE US!!

P. 74 - 119
P. 74

NATURALLY STRAIGHT BLONDE HAIR

RICH

HOW CAN SHE BE JEWISH & LOOK LIKE THAT?!

FAIR SKIN

PUG NOSE

IT'S NOT FAIR IS IT?

COOL & RESERVED

GOOD TASTE

BUT I CAN'T HELP IT I LOVE PEGGY!

TALL (5'1") THIN BODY

LAST NAME LIKE LIPTON

INFATUATED...

WHEN I WAS REALLY YOUNG, I ASKED MY MOM WHY ALL OLD MOVIES WERE IN BLACK AND WHITE. SHE SAID THAT BACK THEN, **EVERYTHING** WAS IN BLACK AND WHITE. I TOOK HER REALLY LITERALLY, AND UNTIL I WAS SIX OR SEVEN, I THOUGHT COLOR WAS SOME WEIRD MODERN INVENTION...

I GUESS

I SPENT A LOT OF TIME AT MY GRANDPARENTS' HOUSE BECAUSE MY MOM HAD TO WORK. I DIDN'T MIND AT ALL, THOUGH. I LIKED BOTH OF MY GRANDPARENTS A LOT.

MY GRANDFATHER WAS RETIRED, BUT HE STILL MAINTAINED A RIGOROUS DAILY SCHEDULE OF YARDWORK: OUTSIDE BY NINE A.M. AND THEN BACK IN AT FIVE TO BATHE, GET DRESSED, WATCH TELEVISION AND EAT DINNER.

SOMETIMES HE'D LET ME HELP HIM DO STUFF, AND THEN WE'D BOTH COME INSIDE TOGETHER AND I'D GET TO TAKE A SHOWER WITH HIM.

THEN WE'D WATCH T.V.

HE HAD SOME STRANGE HABITS. LIKE HE'D REFUSE TO LEAVE THE HOUSE UNLESS HIS UNDERWEAR MATCHED THE COLOR OF HIS CLOTHES.

HE HAD THREE OR FOUR DIFFERENT OUTFITS, EACH ONE WITH MATCHING SHIRT, WALKING SHORTS, BOXER SHORTS, AND SOCKS.

ONCE, MY GRANDMOTHER TOLD ME THIS REALLY FUNNY STORY ABOUT HIM. SHE SAID SHE WAS UP IN THE KITCHEN FIXING DINNER

AND HE WAS IN THE BASEMENT GETTING DRESSED AFTER TAKING HIS SHOWER. SHE HEARD THIS REALLY LOUD

YELP AND SHE RAN TO THE TOP OF THE STAIRS TO SEE WHAT WAS WRONG.

HE SAID THAT HE'D ZIPPED HIMSELF UP IN HIS FLY

AND TOLD HER TO COME DOWNSTAIRS AND HELP

HIM UNDO IT

BUT SHE WOULDN'T, AND TOLD HIM HE SHOULD BE ABLE TO DEAL WITH THINGS LIKE THAT HIMSELF

SO SHE WENT BACK TO COOKING DINNER

AND AFTER ABOUT A HALF AN HOUR OR SO

SHE SAID SHE HEARD ANOTHER LOUD "WHOOP" FROM THE BASEMENT

AND A FEW MINUTES LATER

WITHOUT SAYING A WORD, HE CAME UP THE STAIRS INTO THE KITCHEN, SAT DOWN AT THE TABLE, AND TURNED ON THE TELEVISION.

ONE TIME, WHEN WE WERE WATCHING T.V. TOGETHER

HE SAID SOMETHING ANGRY ABOUT 'COLORED' PEOPLE.

I ASKED HIM WHAT HE MEANT

SINCE HE SAID STUFF LIKE THAT SOMETIMES.

I SAID THAT I THOUGHT THAT EVERYONE WAS 'COLORED', BUT HE SAID THAT I DIDN'T UNDERSTAND.

OUR CLASS WAS IN-VITED TO THIS GIRL'S BIRTHDAY PARTY, AND

BUT HARDLY ANYONE DID. MY BEST FRIEND AND I WERE THE ONLY BOYS THERE.

HER HOUSE MADE ME FEEL FUNNY AND THE HOT DOGS WE HAD FOR DINNER DIDN'T TASTE LIKE THE KIND I WAS USED TO.

I ENDED UP SPENDING THE NIGHT AT MY FRIEND'S HOUSE, AND AFTER

WE'D BEEN LAYING IN BED FOR A LONG TIME

NOT SAYING ANYTHING HE

ASKED ME IF I FELT WEIRD THAT WE WERE THE ONLY BOYS

AT THE PARTY. I SAID NO, AND THEN I

ASKED HIM IF HE FELT WEIRD THAT WE WERE THE ONLY WHITE

KIDS AT THE PARTY. HE SAID NO, AND THEN

HE ASKED ME WHY I SAID THAT. I

REALLY DIDN'T KNOW AND ALL OF A SUDDEN I FELT GROSS SO I ROLLED OVER AND PRETENDED TO GO TO SLEEP.

MY BEST FRIEND

AND I COLLECTED COMIC BOOKS. WE KNEW ALL THE ARTISTS

AND TRIED TO TRACE OUR FAVORITE PICTURES.

HE'D BEEN ON SOME OF THE EARLIEST EXPEDITIONS TO THE SOUTH POLE, AND HE SAVED EVERY MAP, PHOTO, AND PIECE OF CLOTHING HE'D GOTTEN THERE,

A BASEMENT ROOM IN OUR HOUSE JAMMED TO THE CEILING WITH THE STUFF, EXCEPT FOR THESE BIG OLIVE DRAB CANVAS PANTS, A DOWN COAT, AND A PAIR OF

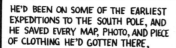

 *mittens*

WHICH HE KEPT BY THE GARAGE.

THOUGH THE WINTERS IN THE MIDWEST WERE CONSIDERABLY LESS HARSH THAN THOSE IN ANTARCTICA,

HE STILL INSISTED ON WEARING ALL OF THIS STUFF WHEN SHOVELING THE WALKS OR EVEN

JUST SCRAPING THE ICE OFF HIS WINDSHIELD.

THIS

REALLY STARTED TO BUG ME,

SINCE HE COULD BARELY MOVE DRESSED LIKE THAT AND LOOKED SORT OF

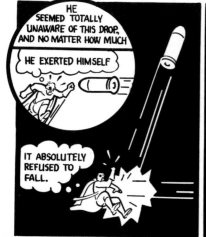

LIKE

A BIG CLOWN.

THE WORST PART, THOUGH, WAS WHENEVER HE WENT OUTSIDE

WEARING THIS STUFF, HIS NOSE WOULD GO NUMB AND DEVELOP A DROP OF

PERFECTLY CLEAR LIQUID AT ITS TIP. IT WAS GROSS.

HE SEEMED TOTALLY UNAWARE OF THIS DROP, AND NO MATTER HOW MUCH

HE EXERTED HIMSELF

IT ABSOLUTELY REFUSED TO FALL.

IT GOT TO THE POINT WHEN WE WERE OUTSIDE TOGETHER WHERE I WOULDN'T LOOK HIM IN THE FACE OR I WOULD PURPOSEFULLY BLUR

MY EYES TO AVOID HAVING TO CATCH A GLIMPSE OF IT.

I REMEMBER THIS ONE TIME AT DINNER. HE WAS TELLING ME

CREEPY THINGS LIKE HE SOMETIMES DID, LIKE HOW

I SHOULD 'LOOK OUT' FOR 'COLORED PEOPLE' BECAUSE THEY WANTED TO 'HURT ME.' MY MOM

SEEMED TO BE GETTING REALLY ANGRY, AND WHEN HE SAID SOMETHING ABOUT HOW

'HITLER WAS RIGHT,' SHE THREW A PLATE AND STARTED YELLING AT HIM.

I DON'T THINK THEY STAYED TOGETHER MUCH LONGER AFTER THAT.

ONE OF THE LAST TIMES I EVER SAW HIM WAS WHEN I SPENT THE NIGHT AT HIS APARTMENT. I REMEMBER FEELING REALLY UNCOMFORTABLE.

HE COOKED DINNER, BUT I DIDN'T EAT MUCH BECAUSE IT WASN'T VERY GOOD.

I DIDN'T SAY VERY MUCH BECAUSE I KNEW HE WANTED US BOTH TO SLEEP IN THE SAME ROOM.

HE SAID HE WANTED US TO TELL STORIES AND JOKES TO EACH OTHER LIKE HE REMEMBERED MY FRIENDS AND ME DOING AT SLUMBER PARTIES,

MAYBE THAT'S WHAT WE DID, BUT I DON'T REMEMBER IT. I GUESS

THAT ACTUALLY WAS THE LAST TIME I EVER SAW HIM.

BUT THAT WAS OKAY WITH ME, SINCE I LIKED THINGS BETTER

WHEN

IT WAS JUST MY MOM AND ME, ANYWAY.

EVERYBODY'S BUDDY

BUDDY RICH TRIO

LAKEWOOD GARDE

BY DREW FRIEDMAN ©1990

DRUMMER *BUDDY RICH...*

WHAT KIND OF PLAYING IS BEING PLAYED HERE? NEW BENDING, NEW PHRASING, NEW SOUNDS. NO TIME. WHAT THE FUCK YOU THINK I'M RUNNING HERE? I'M ACCUSTOMED TO WORKING WITH *NUMBER ONE* MUSICIANS. YOU'RE UP THERE FUCKIN' HIGH SCHOOL BULLSHIT JIVE ARTIST. YOU CAN'T PLAY THE SAME FUCKIN' TUNE. YOU CAN'T HOLD A CHORD. YOU CAN'T PLAY TIME WHEN YOU PLAY SOLO. *FUCK YOU!*

TALKING THINGS OVER WITH HIS TRUMPET PLAYER.

MAKE UP YOUR *FUCKIN'* MIND IF YOU WANT A BEARD OR A JOB. IT'S NOT THE GODDAMN HOUSE OF DAVID. IT'S THE BUDDY RICH BAND. YOUNG PEOPLE WITH FACES. IF YOU DON'T LIKE IT, *GET OUT!* YOU GOT 2 WEEKS TO MAKE UP YOUR FUCKIN' MIND, IF *YOU HAD* A MIND. WHEN YOU GO OUT THERE IF I CATCH THE FUCKIN' BEARD ON YOU, I'LL GIVE YOU A RIGHT HAND TO YOUR *FUCKIN' BRAIN* IF YOU WANT IT. *ASSHOLE.* I'VE PLAYED WITH THE *GREATEST* MUSICIANS IN THE FUCKIN' *WORLD!* I *DON'T NEED THIS SHIT!*

WHAT THE FUCK KIND OF MUSIC DO YOU THINK YOU'RE PLAYING HERE ANYHOW? AND WHO DO YOU THINK YOU'RE PLAYING FOR? I'M UP THERE KNOCKING MY FUCKIN' BRAINS OUT AND I GOT TO CARRY YOU *AND* PAY YOU AT THE SAME TIME... *FUCK YOU...*

LATER, TWO FRIENDS SHARE A DRINK AT THE HOTEL BAR...

WHO'S THE GREATEST FUCKIN' DRUMMER IN THE WORLD?

EPILOGUE

BUDDY RICH DIED IN 1987. A DAY AFTER HIS DEATH, A MUSICIAN WHO HAD PLAYED FOR BUDDY CALLED HIS HOME AND SPOKE WITH HIS WIFE. "IS BUDDY HOME?" THE MAN ASKED. "BUDDY IS DEAD" HIS WIFE ANSWERED. THE NEXT DAY THE MAN CALLED AGAIN. "MAY I SPEAK WITH BUDDY?" HE ASKED. AGAIN HIS WIFE REPEATED "BUDDY IS DEAD." THE NEXT DAY HE CALLED AGAIN. "IS BUDDY IN?" HIS WIFE, NOW CLEARLY ANNOYED, BARKED BACK "THIS IS THE THIRD TIME YOU'VE CALLED ASKING FOR MY LATE HUSBAND. BUDDY IS DEAD." "I KNOW," SAID THE MAN. "I JUST LIKE HEARING IT."

END

THANKS TO AL KOOPER, PAUL BIDUS, JIM McGROGAN AND EDDIE G.

Garish Feline I-VI

PROXY

DOC'S FIRST WIFE WAS A BIG GIRL. NOT FAT, JUST ... **BIG** . BUT THIS GIRL VERNA THAT HE'S MARRYING TODAY? I DON'T KNOW HER. GEEZ ... I DON'T KNOW **DOC** ANYMORE. IT'S BEEN ALMOST SEVEN YEARS.

YOU'D PROBABLY LIKE DOC, JOAN. SURE YOU WON'T CHANGE YOUR MIND AND COME WITH ME?

I'M BUSY, MARTIN. I HAVE THINGS TO DO. AND I **HATE** WEDDINGS!

DOC AND ME USED TO WORK TOGETHER AT THE TOOL-AND-DYE SHOP. HE LIKED HIS FRIED-EGG SANDWICHES. HE DRANK HIS COFFEE BLACK.

HE USED TO ASK ME TO LEND HIM MONEY. I DON'T THINK I EVER TURNED HIM DOWN.

Story: Tom De Haven

Pictures: Richard Sala

WEEKENDS WE'D GO TO YARDSALES TOGETHER, FLEA MARKETS. HE COLLECTED OLD CAMERAS. SOME OF THEM EVEN WORKED.

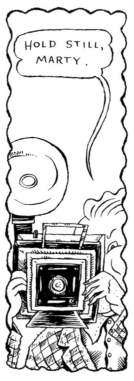

HOLD STILL, MARTY.

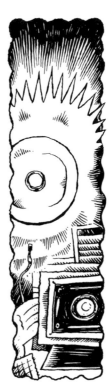

ME? WHY DON'T YOU TELL HER?

YOU'RE NOT LISTENING. IF IT WAS ONLY A MATTER OF BREAKING UP, I'D DO IT. BUT IT'S MORE THAN THAT. I COULD GET MYSELF ARRESTED! SHE FOUND THE PICTURES!

DOC'S FIRST WIFE AND ME GOT ON FINE. I WAS ALWAYS GIVING HER ADVICE. WHENEVER SHE ASKED FOR IT, OF COURSE. I'D TELL HER, "OH, DON'T WORRY ABOUT DOC. JUST HUMOR HIM."

SHE LIKES YOU, MARTY... SO COULD YOU KIND OF SMOOTH THINGS?

WHAT PICTURES ARE YOU TALKING ABOUT?

LISTEN — ARE YOU GONNA DO ME THIS FAVOR OR NOT?

-YEAH, SURE- I'LL TALK TO HER...

SHE WASN'T SURPRISED WHEN I SHOWED UP. SHE SEEMED VERY COMPOSED.

THE PICTURES KIND OF RATTLED ME. I RECOGNIZED SOME OF THE WOMEN FROM WORK. ...

SEE ANYTHING YOU LIKE?

SHE WAS A BIG GIRL... DOC'S FIRST WIFE.

I DON'T KNOW WHY, AFTER ALL THIS TIME, DOC WOULD INVITE ME TO HIS WEDDING.

OR WHY I'D COME...

FRIEND OF...?

THE GROOM.

HOW DO YOU DO? I'M VERNA'S BROTHER, LEO.

4

MARTIN BROWN.

WELL... WELL... WELL... ...SHALL WE GO ON INSIDE?

GEEZ..., IT'S ALMOST FOUR-THIRTY. WHERE'S THE BRIDE? WHERE'S DOC? WHEN'S THIS THING GONNA GET STARTED?!

MARTY? COULD I HAVE A WORD WITH YOU OUTSIDE? I NEED TO ASK A FAVOR.

"FAVOR...?"

"WHAT KIND OF FAVOR?"

"WE HAVE A LITTLE PROBLEM. THE GROOM HAS BEEN ... DELAYED."

"FOR HOW LONG?"

"I'M AFRAID HE WON'T BE ABLE TO MAKE IT AT ALL, MARTY."

"WHY? IS HE SICK?"

"NO, NO! HE'S JUST ... UNABLE TO GET HERE, FROM WHAT I CAN GATHER. IT WAS A BAD CONNECTION ... "

"WHERE THE HELL IS HE?"

"WE DON'T KNOW, BUT IT WOULD BE NICE IF WE DIDN'T HAVE TO POSTPONE ANYTHING."

"...BUT..."

"WE WERE THINKING THAT PERHAPS WE COULD HAVE THE CEREMONY WITHOUT DOC."

...WHICH IS AN HONORABLE ESTATE INSTITUTED BY GOD IN THE TIME OF MAN'S INNOCENCE...

I ALWAYS KNEW DOC WAS A BASTARD. I LOANED HIM MONEY. HE NEVER PAID ME BACK.

... SIGNIFYING UNTO US THE MYSTIC UNION BETWIXT...

JUST THE KIND TO MISS HIS OWN WEDDING.

... IN SICKNESS AND IN HEALTH...

"... FOR AS LONG AS YOU BOTH SHALL LIVE..."

I WILL.

9

THAT WASN'T SO BAD. IT'LL MAKE A GOOD STORY. TELL JOAN, "HEY ~ GUESS WHAT I DID AT DOC'S WEDDING? MARRIED HIS BRIDE!"

...I WONDER IF SHE'LL LAUGH.

MAUS

ART SPIEGELMAN, a cartoonist born after WW II, is planning a book about his parents' lives as Polish Jews during the war. He interviews his father. They don't get along.

VLADEK, his father, lives in Rego Park, NY. He is in poor health. In 1937, in Sosnowiec, he married **Anja**. Their first son, Richieu, died in the war. In 1968, Anja killed herself.

MALA, Vladek's second wife, is also a survivor. Their relationship is stormy. This past summer she has left him.

CHAPTER TEN

SYNOPSIS: In March, 1944, after years in ghettos and in hiding, Vladek and Anja were caught and sent to Auschwitz, where they were separated. Still alive when the camp was evacuated, he was taken to Dachau. "Here," he said, "my troubles began." Starved and weak, he got typhus and almost died. In the Spring he was put on a train to Switzerland...

Back in Rego Park. Late Autumn...

ALWAYS I SAVED...

I SAVED ONLY SO I CAN HAVE A LITTLE SOMETHING FOR MY OLD AGE.

SO, NOW I HAVE MY OLD AGE, AND *LOOK* WHAT I HAVE...

I HAVE A TANK WITH OXYGEN AND I'M SO WEAK WITH MY HEART AND MY DIABETES, I CAN'T LIVE ANYMORE ALONE

I HAVE SO MUCH *ROOM*. YOU AND FRANÇOISE CAN COME AND, FOR NO RENT, LIVE HERE BY ME...

NO! THAT'S TOTALLY OUT OF THE QUESTION.

SO, HOW HAVE I TO LIVE, ARTIE... TELL ME! TO GO TO A *RETIRING* HOME, IT'S NOT FOR ME.

WELL, WHY NOT GET A LIVE-IN NURSE? YOU CAN AFFORD IT.

AND WHAT WILL MY *NEIGHBORS* SAY TO IT IF THEY SEE A WOMAN IS LIVING BY ME!

WHA?? SO HIRE A *MALE* NURSE!

YAH! YOU AND MALA, YOU DON'T KNOW TO *MAKE* MONEY, ONLY TO MAKE IT *DISAPPEAR*!

IF I GIVE ON MALA $100,000 OVER TO HER NAME, *THEN* SHE'LL LIVE AGAIN HERE. *THIS* YOU ADVISE ME?

IT'S UP TO YOU.

MAUS. Chapter Ten: "Saved." © 1991 art spiegelman.

I ONLY DON'T KNOW HOW TO ARRANGE MYSELF... MAYBE TO YOUR ROOM I CAN FIND A TENANT TO TAKE CARE ON ME.

UH-HUH. MAY-BE...

WELL... COME! WE HAVE NOW TO CAR-RY UP MY STORM WINDOWS TO PUT IN.

SHIT. I WAS HOPING YOU'D TELL ME MORE OF YOUR STORY...

THIS WE CAN TALK MAYBE AFTER, BUT ALREADY I'M COLD. I LOSE MON-EY TO HEAT WITH NO STORM WINDOWS.

SIGH.

IN OTHER YEARS I PUT BY NOW THE WINDOWS, THAT I DIDN'T NEED HELP.

LOOK... I'LL DO IT, BUT FIRST, JUST TELL ME MORE ABOUT ANJA.

ANJA? WHAT IS TO TELL? EVERYWHERE I LOOK I'M SEEING ANJA...

FROM MY GOOD EYE, FROM MY GLASS EYE, IF THEY'RE OPEN OR THEY'RE CLOSED, ALWAYS I'M THINKING ON ANJA.

UH, I MEANT WHEN YOU WERE IN DACHAU. WHERE WAS ANJA?

CLIK

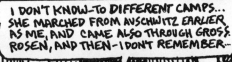

I DON'T KNOW—TO DIFFERENT CAMPS... SHE MARCHED FROM AUSCHWITZ EARLIER AS ME, AND CAME ALSO THROUGH GROSS-ROSEN, AND THEN—I DON'T REMEMBER...

x/2

BUT HOW DID ANJA SURVIVE?

MANCIE-THE HUNGARIAN GIRL WHAT I KNEW THERE IN AUSCHWITZ-SHE KEPT ANJA CLOSE BY TO HER.

AFTER THE WAR I LOOKED ALWAYS FOR MANCIE, TO GIVE A NICE REWARD, BUT I DIDN'T KNOW EVEN HER FULL NAME, AND I NEVER FOUND!

MOM USED TO MENTION RAVENSBRÜCK. WAS MANCIE WITH HER THERE?

YAH... MAYBE IT WAS THERE --

I KNOW ONLY THAT ANJA CAME OUT FREE BY THE RUSSIAN SIDE AND SHE CAME BACK TO SOSNOWIEC BEFORE ME. MY LIBERATION, IT TOOK LONGER...

IT WAS THE LAST MINUTES OF THE WAR, I LEFT DACHAU...

I WENT TO BE EXCHANGED FOR GERMAN PRISONERS ON THE SWISS BORDER BUT WE NEVER CAME.

I REMEMBER WE GOT EACH A TREASURE BOX FROM THE SWISS RED CROSS: SARDINES! BISCUITS! CHOCOLATE!

SOME ATE RIGHT AWAY EVERYTHING. I KEPT, OF COURSE, TO HAVE LATER.

SO, AT NIGHT, SOME TRIED TO STEAL FROM ME....

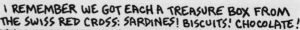

HEY!

WITH MY TYPHUS I NEEDED STILL MUCH TO REST, BUT THIS TREASURE WAS MORE TO ME THAN SLEEPING.

EVERYBODY OUT! LINE UP IN FIVES!

HERE WAS THE END OF OUR RIDE.

WE HAD FROM HERE TO GO BY FOOT TO THE FRONTIER...

AND I SAW, IT'S NOT EVERYWHERE, MY HELL. IT'S STILL LIFE THINGS GOING ON.

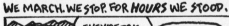

WE MARCH. WE STOP. FOR HOURS WE STOOD.

WHAT'S GOING ON?

THEY'RE TAKING US BACK TO DACHAU!

NO, NO. THE AMERICANS ARE COMING.

IT WAS COMMOTIONS AND RUMORS. THEN SHOUTS:

THE WAR IS OVER!

IT WAS OVER.

MARCH BACK TO THE TRACKS! SCHNELL!

THEY DIDN'T LEAVE US GO, BUT PUT US TO A FREIGHT TRAIN.

THE AMERICANS WILL BE IN THE NEXT TOWN. THEY CAN HAVE YOU.

ON THIS TRAIN NO GUARDS CAME. SO REALLY WE SAW, IT IS OVER NOW.

IN A HALF HOUR THIS TRAIN STOPPED

HEY! THE AMERICANS AREN'T HERE!

WHY WAIT? LET'S GO!

SOME WENT ONE WAY, SOME ANOTHER...

WE DIDN'T KNOW WHERE WE WENT.

HALT OR WE'LL SHOOT!

ALL OF A SUDDEN, IT WAS A WEHRMACHT PATROL!

LITTLE BY LITTLE THEY GOT ALL OF US WHAT WERE GOING TO BE FREE, MAYBE 150 OR 200 PEOPLE OVER IN THE WOODS, BY A BIG LAKE !!!

I DIDN'T UNDERSTAND WHAT IS GOING ON, BUT I WAS AGAIN HERE IN GERMAN HANDS.

THEY GUARDED SO WE COULDN'T GO AWAY.

THERE ARE MACHINE GUNS SET UP ALL AROUND US!

WE OVERHEARD. THEY INTEND TO MURDER EVERY ONE OF US TONIGHT, RIGHT ON THIS SPOT!

IN THE LATER AFTERNOON I WENT OVER CLOSE TO THE EDGE OF THE WATER ...

VLADEK SPIEGELMAN! IS THAT YOU?!

SHIVEK?! YOU'RE ALIVE?

SHIVEK WAS FROM BEFORE THE WAR. A FRIEND FROM BEDZIN, NEAR SOSNOWIEC.

WE SURVIVED EVERYTHING JUST TO GET SHOT WHILE THE WAR ENDS!

I STILL HAVE A LITTLE COFFEE I ORGANIZED. LET'S MAKE A LAST CUP.

LOOK! GET HIM!

SPLASH

ONE OLDER GUY, HE WAS MAYBE 50, JUMPED TO THE LAKE. IT WAS A FAR SWIM.

KBANG! KBANG!

HE MADE IT! DO YOU HAVE THE STRENGTH TO TRY?

JUST STAY NEAR THE WATER. WE CAN ALWAYS TRY IT WHEN THE REAL SHOOTING STARTS.

SO IT CAME NIGHT. WE WERE TERRIBLE FRIGHTENED. WE SAT AND WAITED.

IT WAS CRYING AND PRAYING. SO LONG WE SURVIVED, AND NOW WE WAITED ONLY THAT THEY SHOOT, BECAUSE WE HAD NOT ELSE TO DO.

"LET'S JUMP" IS WHAT HE SAID. AT THE DINNER BREAK LET'S JUMP.

TONY PASSES ME IN THE LINE OF PEOPLE GETTING OFF. THE LADY IS ASLEEP AND THE BUS DRIVER IS TALKING TO SOMEONE ELSE.

AROUND THE CORNER FROM THE STATION WALKS TONY AND I FOLLOW TRYING NOT TO RUN.

"LET'S GO!" HE GRABS MY ARM AND WE'RE TEARING DOWN THE BLACK STREET. TONY AND PAM. THE PERFECT COUPLE.

BY A LIT STORE WINDOW WE STOP. SANTA MOVING HIS ARM UP AND DOWN AND A MIDGET TRAIN RUNNING AROUND HIS LEGS. A KEY SHOP. THE MAN LOOKS AT US AND WE KEEP WALKING.

RAILROAD TRACKS. CHRISTMAS LIGHTS ON CRUDDY HOUSES GETTING CRUDDIER. JUMPING LIGHTS OF T.V.S. NO ONE KNOWS WHERE I AM.

WE MISS THE BUS AND THEY JUST STICK US ON THE NEXT ONE.

YOUR STUFF'S OK. THEY STICK IT ON A SHELF IN A ROOM.

HOW MUCH MONEY YOU GOT?

"I DON'T KNOW" I SAY. "COME ON PAM," HE SAYS. "DON'T YOU WANT US TO BE TOGETHER?" I STOP. "MY MOM." I SAY. "SCREW HER." HE SAYS. "SHE DITCHED YOU." THE ONE TRUTH I TOLD HIM.

FREEZING HANDS ON MY FACE. MY NEW IDENTITY SAYS OK. YEAH OK. MERRY CHRISTMAS MOM.

HE KISSES ME. "YOU'RE A SEXY LITTLE MAMA." BY A BAR HE TELLS ME WAIT ACROSS THE STREET BUT FIRST GIVE HIM FIVE DOLLARS.

I WATCH HIM GO IN THE BAR. RIGHT NOW I COULD RUN FOR IT. I COULD. I COULD RUN RIGHT NOW.

ONE BOTTLE OF WINE. "CHUG A LUG CHUG A LUG" TONY SINGS "MAKES YOU WANNA HOLLER HI-DEE-HO"

TONY TRIES THE DOOR HANDLES OF CARS. ONE OPENS. HIM AND THE SEXY LITTLE MAMA GET IN. HE HOLDS THE BOTTLE TO HER MOUTH LIKE A BABY.

THE FEELING IS FLOATING, FLOATING IN THE FROZEN AIR WITH HER PANTS PULLED DOWN AND THE WARM HARD OF TONY TRYING TO PUSH. CHUG A LUG CHUG A LUG.

THE CAR DOOR OPENS AND HER HEAD FALLS BACK. SHE SEES THE BARE NAKED STREET. A POLICEMAN'S FEET STANDING.

HE PULLS HER OUT ONE WAY AND TONY GOES THE OTHER. TONY'S HANDS GRAB HER THEN PEEL OFF. RED LIGHTS FLASHING. HER PANTS YANK UP. PAM BARFS.

THIS IS THE STORY OF PAM, NOT ME. I WAS BORN TWO DAYS AFTER CHRISTMAS. A NOTHING DAY WHEN PEOPLE ARE SICK OF PRESENTS. OH HOLY NIGHT THE STARS ARE BRIGHTLY SHINING.

THE BEST PART IS THEY NEVER HANDED ME THE PHONE WHEN THEY CALLED MOM. I GUESS SHE JUST DIDN'T ASK TO TALK TO ME.

THE NEXT BUS WAS TOMORROW. THEY TOOK ME TO A LADY'S HOUSE. CAROLYN. SHE CAME TO THE DOOR IN A ROBE.

I SAT ON HER COUCH. ON HER TREE IT WAS ALL BLUE LIGHTS. I WAS BACK IN MY PERSONAL IDENTITY. I COULD TELL BY MY HORRIBLE FEELINGS.

SHE HANDS ME A TOWEL FOR THE SHOWER AND SAYS IF I GOT PENETRATED TO TELL HER NOW. "NO." I SAY. SHE STARES AT ME. "I DIDN'T." SHE POINTS ME TO THE BATHROOM.

IN THE KITCHEN SHE TELLS ME SHE'S SEEN A LOT OF GIRLS LIKE ME. SHE DRAWS THE MAP OF WHERE I WILL END UP WITH HER FINGERS ON THE TABLE.

SHE HAS A DOG, BOOTSIE. "CAN I HOLD HIM?" I SAY. THE SMELL OF A DOG HAS ALWAYS MADE ME FEEL BETTER.

CAROLYN GIVES ME A CHRISTIAN INSTRUCTION BOOK THAT HAS A GIRL ON THE COVER WITH A MESSED UP EXPRESSION. IT'S TIME TO SLEEP. "PRAY AND GO TO SLEEP" SHE SAYS.

IN THE MORNING THE POLICEMAN HOLDS THE SCREEN DOOR OPEN. IN THE CAR HE TELLS ME WHAT HE WOULD DO TO ME IF I WAS HIS KID.

AT A STOPLIGHT I SEE THE STORE WITH THE SANTA. HIS ARM FROZEN STILL. I DON'T NOTICE THE REST OF THE WAY TO THE STATION.

FINALLY COMES THE BUS. THE POLICEMAN TALKS TO THE DRIVER. DON'T WORRY ABOUT IT MISTER. I'M MY TRUE SELF NOW. TOO CHICKEN TO DO ANYTHING.

YOU HAVE TO UNDERSTAND. IT WOULD BE EASY IF SHE WOULD JUST SCREAM AT ME OR HIT ME BUT THAT'S NOT HER WAY. SHE JUST STARES.

BARFING THE WINE WAS NOTHING COMPARED TO BARFING FROM MY MOM. I WILL GET OFF THIS BUS AND SHE WILL NOT SAY ONE WORD TO ME.

OUR FATHER WHO ART IN HEAVEN AT LEAST NOW I GOT MY ANSWER OF WHY SHE DOESN'T WANT ME HERE.

OUR FATHER WHO ART IN HEAVEN, IT WAS MY FAULT FOR EVEN ASKING.

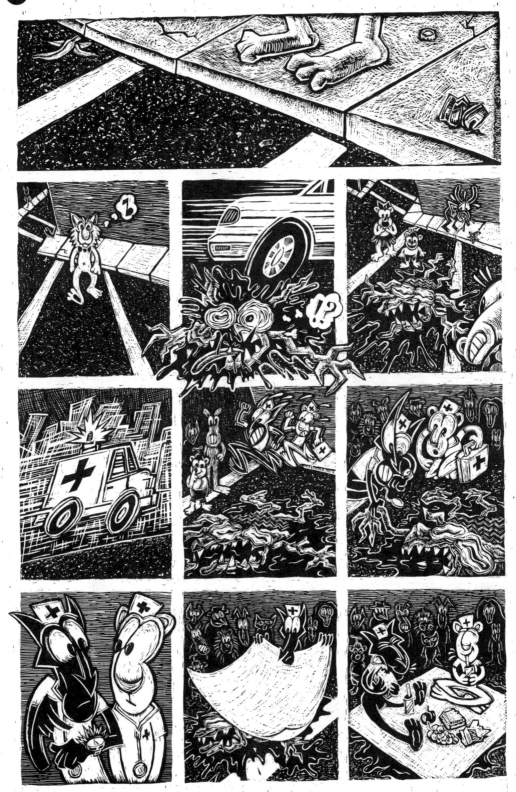

marti

Marti presents **REPULSION**

BENNY BALDON FEELS BEWILDERED AND CONFUSED. HE SEES A DISEMBOWELED PEPA PEREZ LYING ON THE GROUND, HER BLOOD SPURTING OUT, AND HE FEELS AS IF IT NEVER HAPPENED, AS IF HE WASN'T THE PERSON WHO FIRED THE TWO SHOTS THAT KILLED HIS LOVER, RIGHT THERE, IN THE SUPERMARKET PARKING LOT.
WHO WOULD HAVE PREDICTED THAT ALL THE HAPPINESS THEY SHARED WOULD END LIKE THIS... IN A SENSELESS SLAUGHTER...

WHEN THEY FIRST MET AND STARTED DATING, BENNY COULD NOT BELIEVE HIS LUCK... AN OLD MAN OF ALMOST 60 ENJOYING A TENDER YOUNGSTER OF ONLY 37...

TIMES WERE HARD AND LONELY FOR BENNY AFTER HE LEFT THAT UNBEARABLE MONSTER OF A WIFE... UNTIL THE NIGHT HE SAW PEPA AT THE CLUB... WHAT A MONUMENTAL WOMAN!

AAH

IT WAS LIKE A DREAM... HE SIMPLY COULD NOT BELIEVE HIMSELF... HE FELT LIKE THE STUD HE USED TO BE IN THE OLD DAYS... MAKING LOVE END-LESSLY, MAKING HER HAPPIER EACH TIME, EMPTYING HIS LOVE AMONG PASSIONATE HEAVINGS... IT SEEMED LIKE A DREAM...
...BUT IT WAS TRUE...

Translation by Eduardo Kaplan. Lettering by R. Sikoryak.

HIS EARS ARE RINGING... DEAFENED BY THE TWO BLASTS, HE CAN'T HEAR THE TERRIFIED SCREAMS OF THE PASSERSBY AND THE CARS DRIVING BY.

HIS ANGER BECOMES AN ELECTRICAL CURRENT MOVING UP AND DOWN HIS BODY, CAUSING A LIGHT GENERAL TREMBLING.

CLACK—

...YET HE IS ABLE TO UN-LOAD THE TWO SHELLS HE USED AGAINST PEPA.

WHEN SHE SUDDENLY TOLD HIM IT WAS OVER HE WENT MAD.

IT DIDN'T TAKE HIM LONG TO FIND THE REASON... SHE WAS GOING OUT WITH ANOTHER GUY ...A YOUNGER SON OF A BITCH... 50 OR 50-SOMETHING...

IT WAS THE END... AT HIS AGE WOMEN LIKE PEPA WERE HARD TO FIND...

SUDDENLY, HE LONGED FOR THE GOOD TIMES, WHEN SHE WOULD BE SO SENSUAL AND TENDER...SO WILLING TO PLEASE HIM...THE TIMES WHEN SHE WOULD RADIATE THAT YOUTHFUL SPIRIT HE FELT SO ATTRACTED TO...

HE IMAGINES HER AS AN OLD WOMAN...FULL OF THE WRINKLES THAT LOVE CON-CEALS ...AFTER ALL, A 37 YEAR OLD WOMAN IS NOT A CHILD ANYMORE...

AND NOW SHE IS LYING ON THE GROUND...IN A POOL OF BLOOD WITH HER GUTS STICK-ING OUT...RIGID AND FLACCID AT THE SAME TIME... LIKE A BROKEN DOLL...

OBLIVIOUS TO HIS SURROUNDINGS, BENNY LOADS TWO NEW SHELLS INTO HIS SHOTGUN AS HE LEANS AGAINST A WALL...

SLOWLY, HE TURNS THE SHOTGUN ON HIMSELF...

CLACK!

...HOLDING THE DOUBLE BARREL WITH ONE HAND WHILE THE OTHER PULLS ONE OF THE TRIGGERS...

BLAM

CONFUSED BY HIS ANGER, BENNY FORGETS TO PUT THE BARREL IN HIS MOUTH, AND THE BLAST DESTROYS HIS JAW, LIPS, NOSE, AND ONE EYE, COMPLETELY DISFIGURING HIS FACE.

3

THE SECOND BLAST ONLY WORSENS THE MISTAKE HE MADE WITH THE FIRST, SHATTERING THE OTHER EYE AND COMPLETING THE DESTRUCTION OF HIS FACE WITHOUT CAUSING ENOUGH HARM TO ALLOW BENNY TO FALL UNCONSCIOUS...

BLAM

... FEELING HIS CHEST, HE IS SURPRISED TO FIND OUT HE IS STILL ALIVE, AND STANDING...

THEN HE PULLS A BIG KNIFE FROM AN INSIDE POCKET...

AND GATHERING STRENGTH HE STICKS IT IN HIS LEFT LUNG WITH A SOLID BLOW — CHACK!

4

TOTALLY DEVOID OF REASON, BENNY TOUCHES HIS CHEST AND FEELS HIS KNIFE STUCK INSIDE IT...HE CAN'T UNDER- STAND WHY HE IS STILL ALIVE AND STANDING...

INSTINCTIVELY, HE PULLS OUT THE KNIFE COVERED WITH BLOOD...

...AND STICKS THE BLADE AGAIN, THIS TIME IN HIS STOM- ACH WITH ANOTHER SOLID BLOW

CHACK!

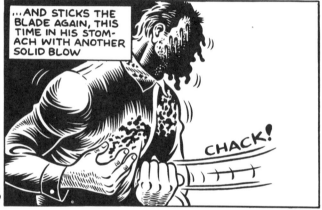

GRABBING IT BY THE HANDLE, BENNY TURNS THE BLADE INSIDE HIM AND FEELS HOW HIS INNARDS CONTRACT AND DILATE AS THE SHARP BLADE CUTS THROUGH THEM...

5

...BENNY DOESN'T FALL... HIS LIFE REFUSES TO ABANDON HIM...

HE PULLS THE KNIFE AGAIN, GASPING FOR AIR DUE TO A DE-STROYED LUNG...

WITHOUT ANY STRENGTH LEFT TO HOLD IT, THE KNIFE FALLS FROM BENNY'S HAND AND HE IS DISARMED, UNABLE TO FINISH HIS SUICIDE...

DANIEL! GET OUT OF THERE!

WHAT'S HAPPENING TO THAT MAN, MOMMA?

—DON'T LOOK!!

PEOPLE SURROUND THE DYING MAN TO WATCH THE HORRIBLE SPECTACLE...

6

END

SOMEBODY SHOOTS THE HORRIBLE SCENE ON VIDEO AND THAT NIGHT BENNY BECOMES A CELEBRITY WHEN HE APPEARS ON THE EVENING NEWS WHILE FAMILIES ARE HAVING DINNER AT HOME... THE VIEWERS WILL BE OVERCOME BY AN ANGUISHED CHILL FOR A FEW SECONDS BEFORE THEY GO BACK TO WOLF DOWN THEIR DINNER, UNAWARE THAT MANY OF THEM WILL HAVE NIGHTMARES THICK WITH RED BLOOD THAT WILL PARCH THEIR MOUTHS AND DARKEN THEIR SPIRITS A LITTLE MORE...

Translation by Elizabeth Bell, F.M. & a.s.   Thanks to David Kunzle, author of *The History of the Comic Strip: The Nineteenth Century* (University of California Press. 1990).

A FULFILLING CAREER Gustave Doré, 1852

As a mere child I drew pictures that my schoolmates fought over, creating an uproar in my class.

In high school I was noted for my talent in caricaturing the teachers.

Always continuing to practice my talents, I got a unanimous verdict on my graduation exams: thumbs down.

My father, who had no artistic leanings whatsoever, did not appreciate my burgeoning skills. He had me drafted. I became Decorator-in-chief of the guardhouse.

I kept the barracks in stitches at the expense of the higher-ups,

...who were not amused,

...and gave me time to continue my studies in solitary.

I hit on the idea of offering my services to Aubert, publisher of humorous periodicals.

I was received by a distinguished gentleman who praised me highly and told me I had considerable aptitude.

Thus I published a few character studies of my fellow Guardsmen and their impressive bearing,

...of the (so-called) "mounted" patrol,

...of facial types among the ranks,

...and among the officers.

My studies of the National Guard earned me a minor court case and a major fine.

After my scientific research into military physiognomy led to several duels, I decided to abandon my career in the military in favor of the less perilous domain of portraying society at large.

I turned to the world of politics, and found it so boring I at once turned elsewhere.

I next turned my attention to the world of literary salons... but found no character to study. Those people all looked alike.

I rendered scenes of everyday life, but that genre is considered repellent and no one bought my work.

Today I apply my skills in Clichy's debtors prison.

OBSERVATION:

I now understand – rather late, but better late than never – that I mistook my raw talent for developed skill, that I settled for being good-enough rather than striving for the Ultimate.

MORAL:

Talent is a precious seed,
but it must be cultivated.